ANCIENT EGYPT
ADVENTURE
Activity Book

Illustrated by Jen Alliston

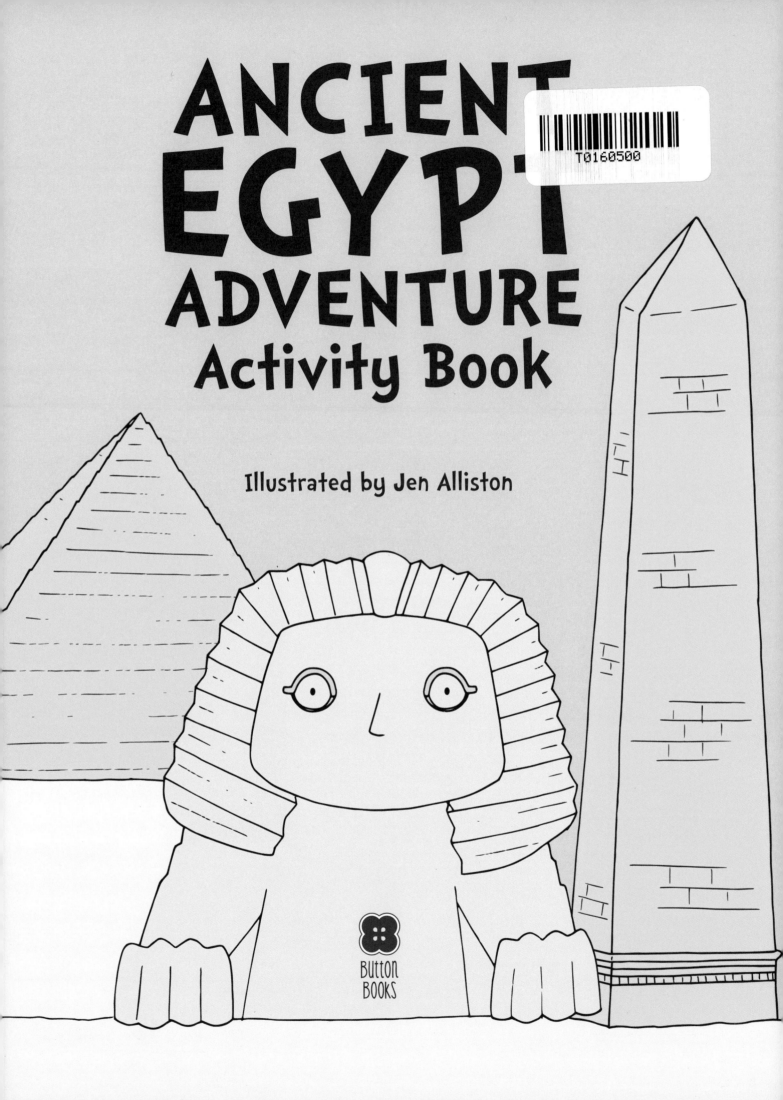

Button
BOOKS

The Ancient Egyptians lived in the lands around the Nile River thousands of years ago. This book has loads of puzzles, mazes, things to make, coloring activities, stickers, and games galore to help you find out more about their world. There are fascinating pharaohs, great gods, puzzling pyramids, and menacing mummies. Get ready for some fantastic fun!

Meet the pharaoh

The king or queen of Egypt was called the pharaoh. Can you use these descriptions to number the different parts of this pharaoh's outfit?

❶ Eyeliner

Pharaohs ringed their eyes with black makeup to protect against eye disease and bright sunlight.

❷ Crook and flail

A shepherd's crook and a rod used to thresh grain were symbols of power.

❸ Headdress

A blue and gold striped headcloth (the Nemes headdress) kept the sun off the pharaoh's head.

❹ Uraeus

The gold cobra (uraeus) that held the headdress in place was a symbol of power.

❺ Tunic

A lightweight, white linen robe kept the pharaoh cool.

❻ False beard

Because Egypt was so hot, pharaohs shaved off all their hair. They wore thin and pointy false beards on special occasions to look like the god Osiris. Even female pharaohs wore a beard!

Odd Osiris out

The Ancient Egyptians believed in life after death. The god Osiris was the ruler of the dead. Which is the odd one out? Color them all to match the god on page 7.

Work it out

Unscramble the words to discover what these Ancient Egyptians did for a living.

RAFERM

_ _ _ _ _ _

VESAL

_ _ _ _ _

PRIEST
SCRIBE
SOLDIER
FARMER
SLAVE

PESTIR

_ _ _ _ _ _

BISCER

_ _ _ _ _ _

DRESOIL

_ _ _ _ _ _ _

Great gods

Ancient Egyptians had gods for nearly everything! Can you match these to their descriptions below?

_ _ _ _ _   _ _ _ _ _ _   _ _ _ _ _ _

Thoth
The god of writing and knowledge. Here, Thoth has the head of an ibis (a bird with a thin beak), but sometimes he has the head of a baboon. He is wearing the blue and gold Nemes headdress.

Bastet
Cat-headed goddess of joy, the home, and childbirth. She is holding a rattle in one hand and an ankh in the other. (An ankh is a cross with an oval loop at the top.)

Anubis
The god of embalming (preserving dead bodies). He has the head of a jackal (a type of wild dog) and is wearing the Nemes headdress.

- - - - - - -　　　　- - - - - - -　　　　- - - - - - -

Osiris
Green-skinned ruler
of the dead. He has a
pointy beard and a
white crown, and holds
a crook and flail.

Isis
Goddess of love and
magic, Isis is the wife
of Osiris and mother of
Horus. She is wearing a
blue mini throne on her
head and a red dress,
and she carries an ankh.

Horus
Hawk-headed god of
honesty and justice. He is
wearing a red and white
double crown. He is also
holding an ankh, which is
a symbol of life.

How to make a water clock

Ancient Egyptians used water clocks to measure the time. Make your own clepsydra (water clock) by following the instructions below.

Ask a grown-up to help!

You'll need:

large, clear plastic bottle

scissors

stopwatch

marker pen

food coloring

4 pints of water

pair of compasses

1. Cut the bottle in half using the scissors.

2. Unscrew the top of the bottle and make a hole in it using the pair of compasses. Then put the lid back on the bottle.

3. Turn the top half of the bottle upside down and place it inside the bottom half.

4. Add a few drops of food coloring to the water.

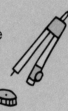

5. Pour the water into the top of the bottle and start timing. Make a mark on the side of the bottle every time a minute passes until all the water is in the bottom part.

6. Your water clock is now complete. To use it, pour the water back into the top and count off the minutes as the water trickles down into the bottom part.

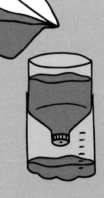

Battle scene counting

How many of the following can you find?

Bows =

Arrows =

Battle axes =

Daggers =

Tall order

Can you put these workers in size order? Number them from 1 for the smallest to 5 for the tallest.

Along the Nile River

You'll find stickers of boats, hippos, crocodiles, and people in the middle pages of this book. Add them to this picture to bring it to life.

Hidden in the pyramid

Can you find all these words related to pyramids?

CHAMBER
SARCOPHAGUS
MUMMY
PHARAOH
STONE
TOMB
DESERT
CURSE
EMBALM
MASK

```
                    C
                   R U E
                  S L R N A
                 U S K S M I O
                D I A M E U P Y R
               M O T R A S W M D A L
              J Q R Y C H A M B E R O P
             M S M L K O W E N M S B Y L M
            A U Q G W U P T M K J E J D U A R
           M Y M W T N R H L R O I R M M M S N L
          B K N M E H M F A D S S U T M M T K B P O
         A O G O Y T J D H G Q M P H A R A O H Z Q I K
        R S D H T P C S U J U H M D R T P H M L V U R J L
       E M B A L M G N Z M E S T O N E B L M B M C M T G K J
```

Dog differences

Ancient Egyptians loved dogs. Find five differences between these two dog statues.

Chariot math

Which chariot is going to win the race? Do the math to find out and write the answers in the circles. The one with the highest number will be the winner.

$6 - 4 + 2 =$

$6 - 3 - 1 =$

$4 + 4 - 2 =$

Odd beetle out

Which of these scarab beetles is the odd one out? When you've worked that out, color them all in.

Egyptian bracelets

Ask a grown-up to help!

You'll need:

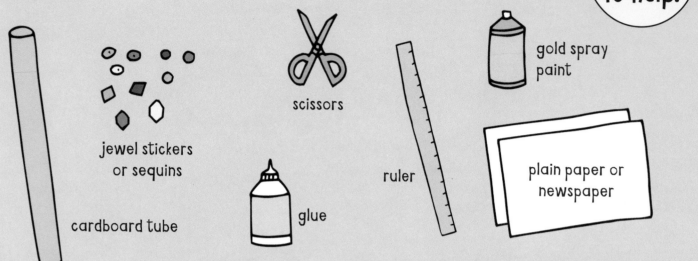

jewel stickers or sequins

cardboard tube

scissors

glue

ruler

gold spray paint

plain paper or newspaper

1. Cut your cardboard tube into pieces about 2in wide.

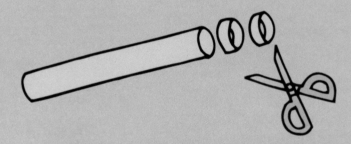

2. Snip one side of each piece to make an opening.

3. Spray each bracelet with gold paint and leave to dry. (Do this on some newspaper or plain paper.)

4. Stick on some jewels or sequins to decorate your bracelets.

5. Put them on!

Where's my mummy?

This menacing mummy is fading away! Draw it back in, then color in the rest of the picture.

Tomb raider

Help the archaeologist find her way to the treasure at the center of the pyramid.

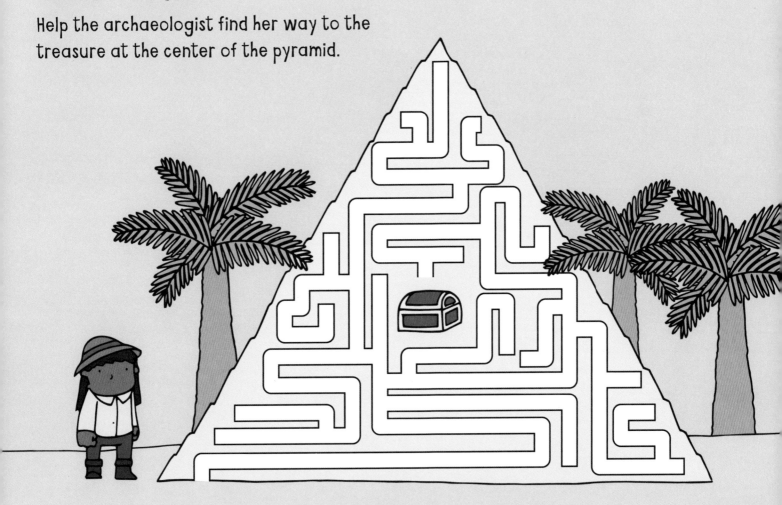

Find the lost tomb

Follow the clues below to find the lost tomb of King Akhenaten. Draw your route on the picture and mark the spot with an X.

Start at the Great Temple.

Cross the river and go to the Temple of the Sun.

Go back across the Eastern Desert and cross the river to the Valley of the Pharaohs.

Cross back over the river to the Oasis.

Go around the Obelisk and cross over the river to the Sphinx.

Mark your X between the Sphinx and the Giant Pyramid.

Mystery case

What's missing from the archaeologist's trunk? Using the list below, can you work out what she's forgotten to pack?

Spade
Camera
Sunglasses
Flashlight
Sketch book
Pencil
Map
Tape measure
Water bottle
Compass

Ancient jokes

Who changed the baby pharaoh's diaper?
His mummy.

Why was the pharaoh only 12 inches tall?
He was just an average ruler.

How do brave Egyptians write?
With heroglyphics.

What do you get in a luxury pyramid?
A tomb with a view.

Soldiering on

Can you spot five differences between these two soldiers?

Odd shields out

Which three shields are different from the rest? Color them all in.

Animal pairs

These feature in stories about Ancient Egypt. Find the pairs and color them in to match.

Top of the pile

Do the math to work out which is the highest pyramid and write your answers in the circles below. Then color them in if you like.

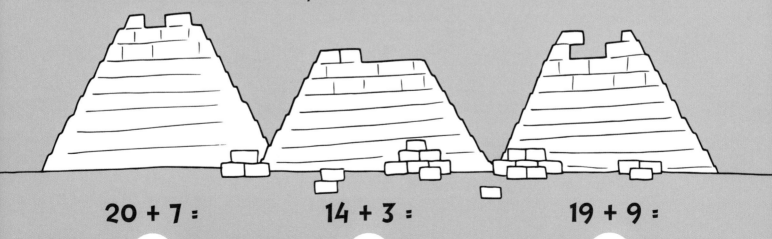

20 + 7 =

14 + 3 =

19 + 9 =

Dotty sphinx

Join the dots to show this super sphinx, then color it in if you like.

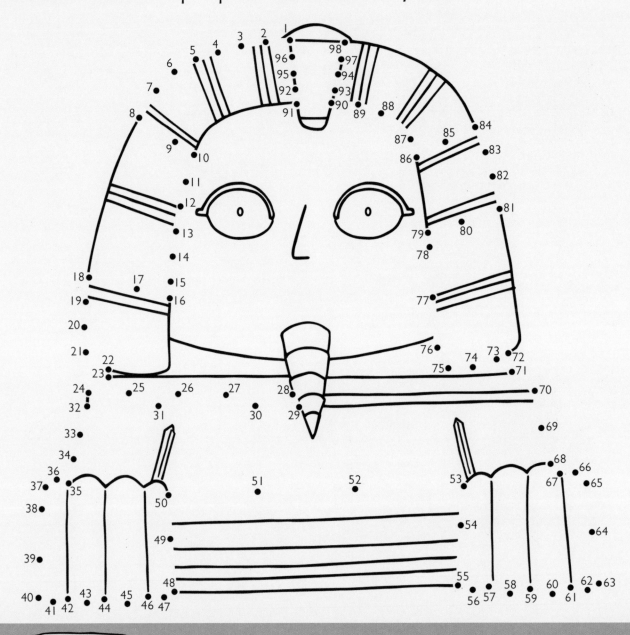

Recycled letters

Can you complete these words using all the letters in the word EMBALM?

to_b   curs_

scri_e   s_ave

pyra_id   fl_il

Muddled animal gods

Can you work out what these sacred animals are?

coolicred _ _ _ _ _ _ _ _ _

tac _ _ _

lackaj _ _ _ _ _ _ _

anolfc _ _ _ _ _ _ _

onobab _ _ _ _ _ _ _

shipaptompuo _ _ _ _ _ _ _ _ _ _ _ _

baboon

hippopotamus

crocodile

jackal

cat

falcon

Cattle counting

Help the scribe count the cattle. How many horns can you see?

Cattle ◯   **Horns** ◯

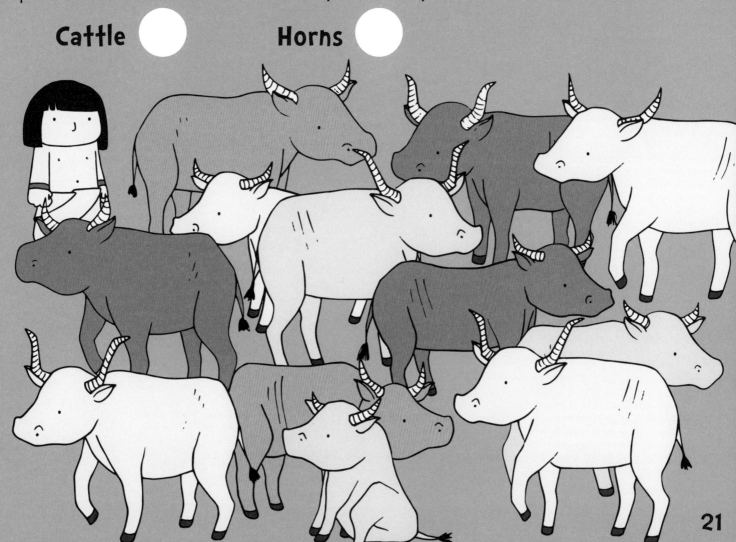

High and mighty

Use some stickers to decorate this scene of the pyramids.

Super symbols

The Ancient Egyptians used a system of picture writing called hieroglyphics.
Pictures represented letters of the alphabet (V and W had the same one).

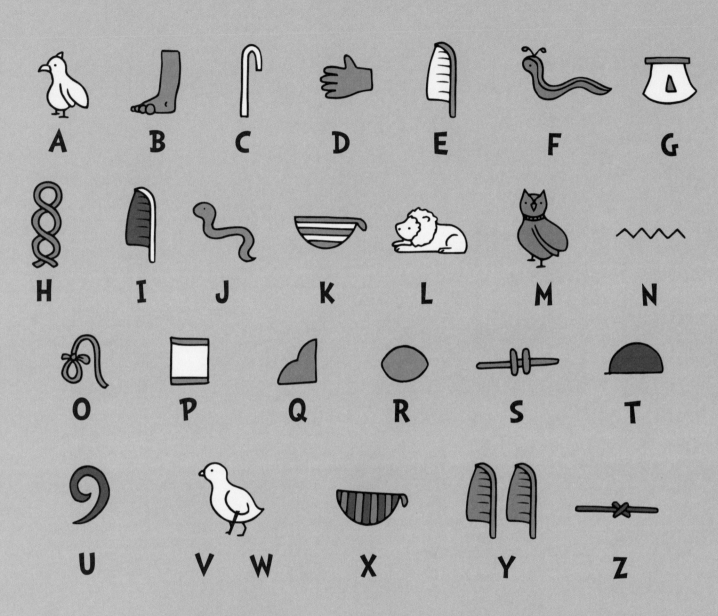

Write your name using the hieroglyphics.

Secret message

Queen Cleo is worried that her enemies are going to attack, so she has sent her friend Mark Antony a secret message. Some of the letters have been left out. Can you work out what the message says from the list of words underneath?

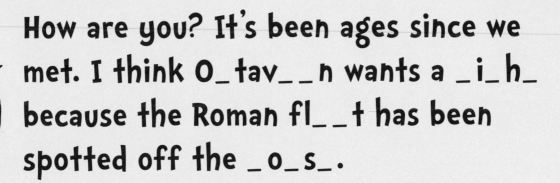

Dear Mark Antony,

How are you? It's been ages since we met. I think O_tav__n wants a _i_h_ because the Roman fl__t has been spotted off the _o_s_.

Please bring as many _hi_s as you can and come q_ic_ly!

Love, Cleo

FIGHT   **COAST**

OCTAVIAN   **QUICKLY**

SHIPS   **FLEET**

Make a hieroglyphics tablet

Make a "stone" tablet and write a word on it using the alphabet pictures on page 24. When dry, you could varnish the tablet to make it waterproof.

on page 24

Ask a grown-up to help!

You'll need:

measuring cup

2 cups flour

³/₄ cup water

large mixing bowl

2 tbsp glue

3 cups sand

rolling pin

plastic wrap

wooden spoon

plastic knife or lollipop stick

1. Put the flour into a large mixing bowl and mix the water into the flour until it forms a sticky dough.

2. Pour 2 cups of sand over the dough and use your fingers to work it into the dough.

3. Make a well in the center of the dough ball and add the glue. Knead the dough ball again to spread the glue.

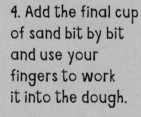

4. Add the final cup of sand bit by bit and use your fingers to work it into the dough.

5. Spread the plastic wrap on your work surface and turn out the dough ball onto it. Flatten the ball with your fist and shape it into a rectangle with a rolling pin until it's about ½in thick.

6. Cut it into rectangles, and carve your hieroglyphics directly onto it using the knife or lollipop stick. If you make a mistake, smooth out the marks with your fingers and write the symbol again.

7. Leave your tablet in a warm place to dry out. Turn over after a few hours to dry the other side.

Game play

Can you spot five differences between these two pictures of people playing Senet, an ancient board game?

Royal coloring

Color in the queen and her ceremonial chair. The chair was made of gold and used on special occasions as a symbol of royal power.

Marvelous mask

Follow the key and color in King Tut's funeral mask:

1 = Gold/yellow

3 = Green

2 = Blue

4 = Red

Plain sailing

Do the math to see which is the fastest felucca (an ancient wooden sailing boat). Write your answers in the circles. The highest number is the fastest boat.

$8 + 1 - 5 =$

$4 + 6 - 3 =$

$12 - 2 + 4 =$

Market dash

Help the slave get to the market before it sells out of fish!

Party time

The queen and her friends are getting ready for a feast.
Use the stickers to dress them up.

Dance differences

Which two of these dancers are the odd ones out?

Musical mayhem

Can you work out which instrument belongs to which musician? Follow the tangled lines to find out who's going to play the tambourine, lute (a type of guitar), and trumpet.

Tambourine

Lute

Trumpet

On the menu

What did the Ancient Egyptians like to eat and drink? Circle the words hidden in the puzzle to find out.

LENTILS

FISH

GARLIC

FIGS

DATES

BREAD

BEER

HONEY

EGGS

CHEESE

R M U C L K R U X R Y S T M C A R N O
B H O N E Y P L C A A F I S H P B Y X
V I B E Y R F M Y S T S T D E L A R E
C P D D L H J N G N N S T H E E K H T
K K L S E T G F I O E B H U S S B O A
O L I W N V R N Z P V G R I E N W H S
R L M S T B S I F I G S J F M X A E S
Y Q R P I N A F P O E A E K B Y B J L
D S H O L L G N U C X K L Q K R K A D
A E G G S A E K J Y M F O W T E T F A
E M E Q I T S N B T B E E R A E V I T
T B J S G X G F E R P O R E Z A M U E
U L K G A R L I C Z A S B R E A D N S

Make a decorated collar

You'll need:

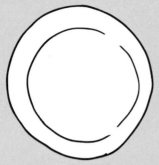

large paper plate,
approx. 10in diameter

 pencil

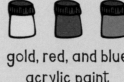 gold, red, and blue
acrylic paint

Ask a grown-up to help!

 scissors

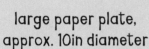 small saucer or other round object, approx. 6in diameter

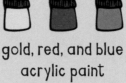 paintbrushes

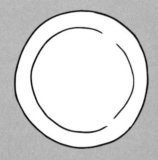 1. Place the paper plate face down on a work surface.

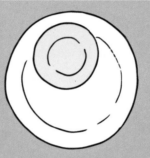 2. To make an opening for the neck, place the saucer in the center about 1in from the top edge of the paper plate. Draw around the saucer to mark out a circle.

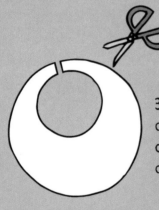 3. Cut along the outline of the inner circle and cut a vertical slit to the outside edge.

 4. Try the collar on to see if it fits. Trim the ends and widen the circle if it's too tight.

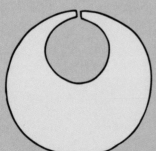 5. Paint the collar gold and leave to dry.

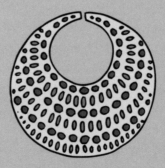 6. Paint alternating rows of color until the whole collar is decorated.

7. Leave to dry, then wear it!

hole chariots treasure jewels

flashlight gold fortune furniture

coins pharaoh

Dotty queen

Cats were popular pets in Ancient Egypt and were worshipped as gods. Join the dots to complete this picture of Queen Cleo and her feline friends, then color them in.

Off to the royal tomb

Add some stickers to this funeral procession.

Make an Ancient Egyptian headband

Ask a grown-up to help!

You'll need:

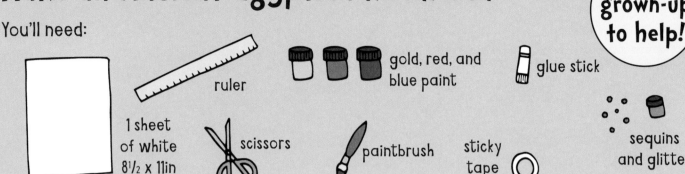

1 sheet of white 8½ x 11in card stock

ruler

scissors

gold, red, and blue paint

paintbrush

sticky tape

glue stick

sequins and glitter

cobra template

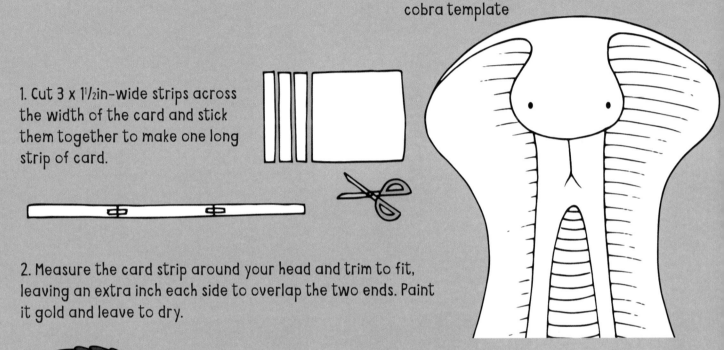

1. Cut 3 x 1½in-wide strips across the width of the card and stick them together to make one long strip of card.

2. Measure the card strip around your head and trim to fit, leaving an extra inch each side to overlap the two ends. Paint it gold and leave to dry.

3. Photocopy the cobra template and glue it onto the remaining piece of card. Cut out.

4. Paint the cobra piece with gold, red, and blue paint as shown. Leave to dry, then stick in the middle of the long card strip.

5. If you like, decorate the long strip with sequins and glitter. Leave to dry, then tape the ends of the headband together.

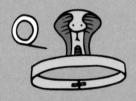

6. Wear your headband!

Weighing it up

The Ancient Egyptians believed that your heart was weighed by the god Anubis after you died. If it weighed less than a feather, you could enter the afterlife. Do the math to find out which of these hearts will pass the test. The lowest number wins.

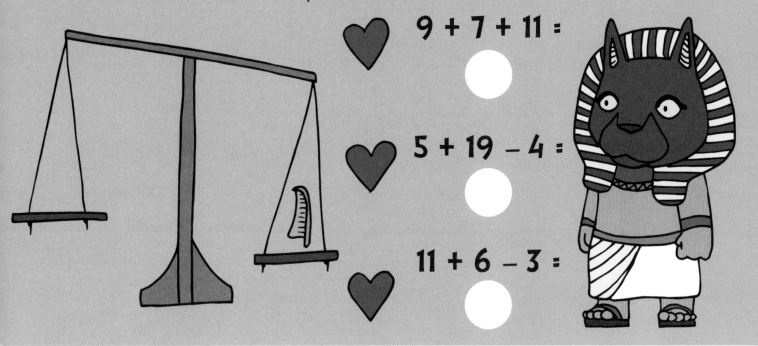

$9 + 7 + 11 =$ ◯

$5 + 19 - 4 =$ ◯

$11 + 6 - 3 =$ ◯

Mirror image

Draw in the other half of these Ancient Egyptians, then color them in.

Temple run

Help the priest find the way to the temple.
Don't forget to pick up the book of spells on the way!

Odd cats out

Which two of these cat statues are the odd ones out?

Ceremonial dress up

Color in these temple priests. How many people are wearing animal skins?

The write stuff

Can you spot five differences between these two pictures of scribes?

Bottling it up

After death, the pharaoh's stomach, lungs, guts, and liver were kept in special containers called canopic jars, so they could be used in the afterlife. Color these jars in.

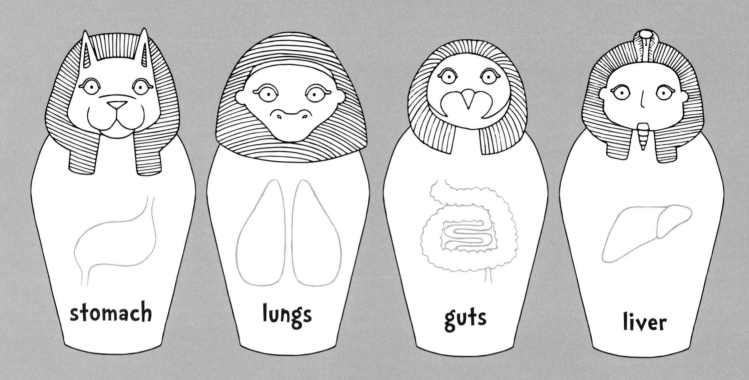

stomach   lungs   guts   liver

Tomb treasure

Someone who studies Ancient Egypt is called an Egyptologist. Choose words from the sticker pages and complete the diary entry to see what this one found.

Today I cut a hole in the secret door. I held up my [_____] and looked

through the [_____]. I couldn't believe my eyes! The room was filled with

[_____]. There were statues, enormous vases, and [_____], all

made of [_____]. There were heaps of [_____] and piles of gold

[_____]. There was a small boat to carry the [_____] to the

Underworld. That too was made of gold. Hooray! I had found a fortune.

Making a mummy

A pharaoh's body was embalmed (preserved) after death to stop it from rotting. The insides were removed and the body was cleaned, dried out, and wrapped in bandages. Check the list to see what's missing from the picture.

Natron (salt)

Bandages

Mask of Anubis

Needle and thread

Book of the Dead

Canopic jars

Soap

Spoon

Knife

Iron hook

Wine

Stop, thief!

Who stole the pharaoh's treasure? Follow the tangled lines to find out.

Hidden in the picture

This naughty slave has hidden King Tut's collar, sandals, crook, flail, and musical instrument. Can you spot them?

Name game

A cartouche is an oval name plate that was put on the pharaoh's coffin so everyone knew who was in there! Can you spot five differences between these two cartouches?

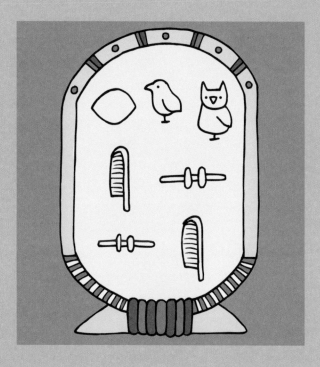 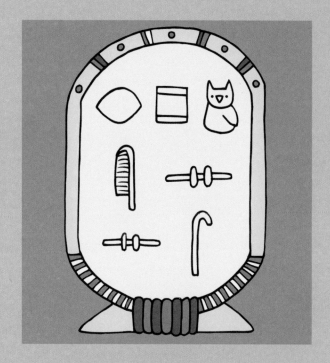

Twin charms

Match the pairs of amulets (good luck objects), then color them in.

Make a pharaoh's beard

Make a false beard so you can look like Osiris, lord of the Underworld!

Ask a grown-up to help!

You'll need:

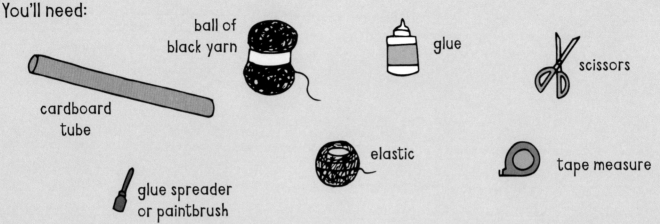

ball of black yarn

cardboard tube

glue

scissors

glue spreader or paintbrush

elastic

tape measure

1. Cut the cardboard tube so it's about 6in long. Spread a layer of glue all over it.

2. Starting at one end of the tube, wrap black yarn around it all the way to the other end.

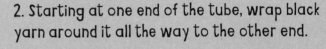

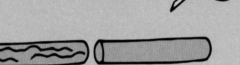

3. When the glue has dried, use the scissors or a pencil to make a small hole either side of the tube, about ³/₄in from one end.

4. To make a chin strap, cut a length of black elastic about 24in long. It should be long enough to go around the back of your head, around your ears, and meet under your chin. Push one end of the elastic through one hole and tie a knot in the end.

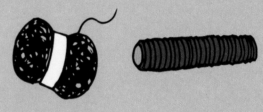

5. Push the other end of the elastic through the other hole and fit over your head, wrapping around your ears, and tie a knot in the other end of the elastic. Now wear your beard!

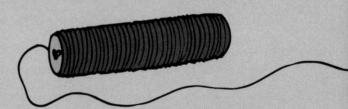

45

Journey through the Underworld

Help the pharaoh's spirit travel through the Underworld to reach Osiris in the Hall of Judgment. Make sure he doesn't get eaten by Sobek, the crocodile god, on the way!

Heavy weights

The Ancient Egyptians were very clever at moving heavy objects. Who will reach the pyramid building site first? Do the math and write the answers in the circles. The highest number is the winner.

$$15 + 7 - 4 =$$

$$6 - 4 + 13 =$$

$$13 - 4 + 15 =$$

High society

One of these men has just become the new pharaoh. He has a pointy beard and is carrying an ankh in his right hand (a cross with a loop at the top). Work out who he is, then color him and his friends in.

Inside King Tut's tomb

Add stickers to decorate the inside of King Tut's tomb.

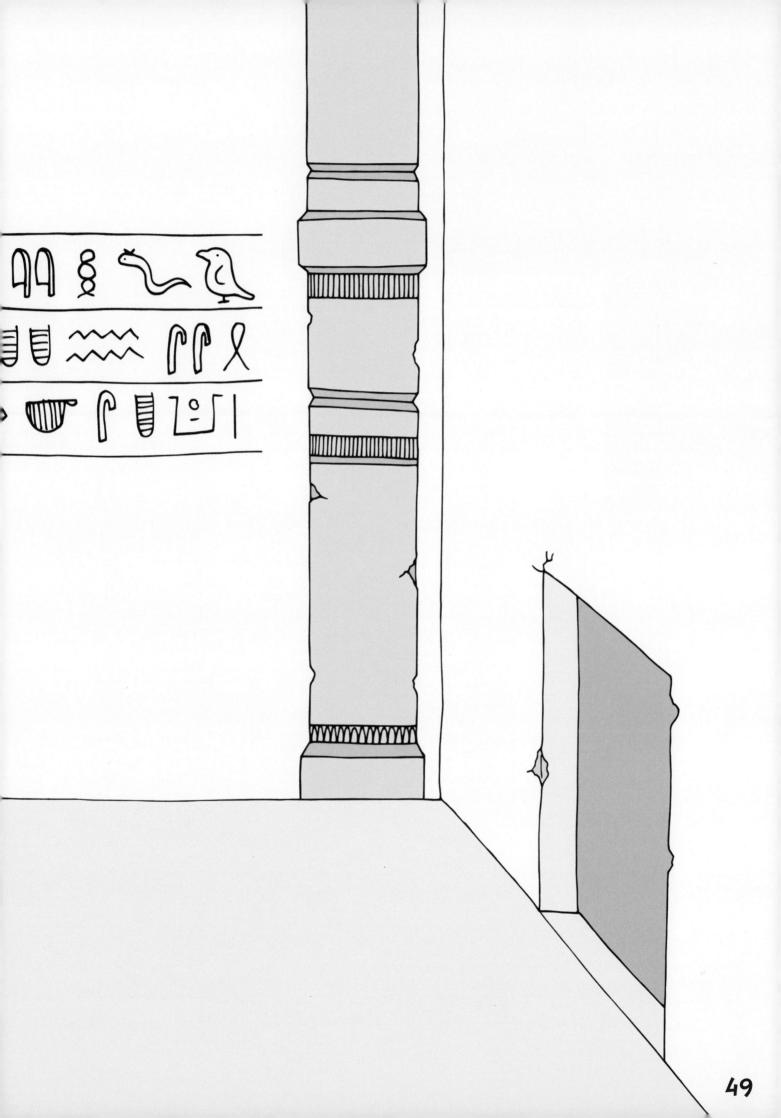

49

Figure it out

Join the dots to reveal this figure guarding the Great Temple.
Color it in and add some stickers too, if you like.

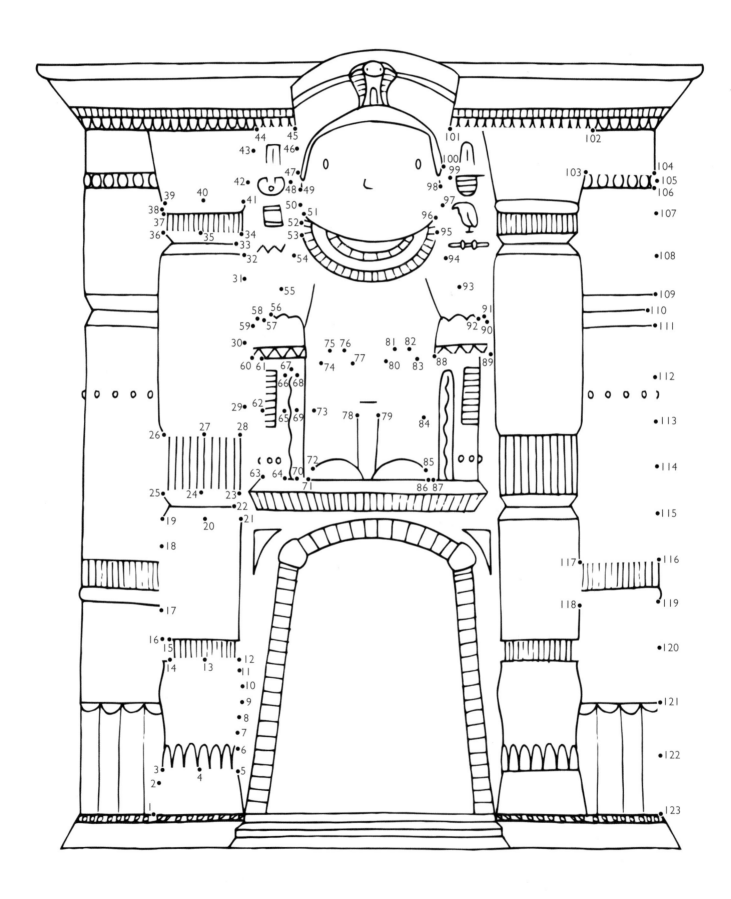

Gods wordsearch

See if you can find these gods and goddesses in the wordsearch:

AMUN

ANUBIS

BASTET

BES

HAPI

HATHOR

HORUS

ISIS

SET

TAWARET

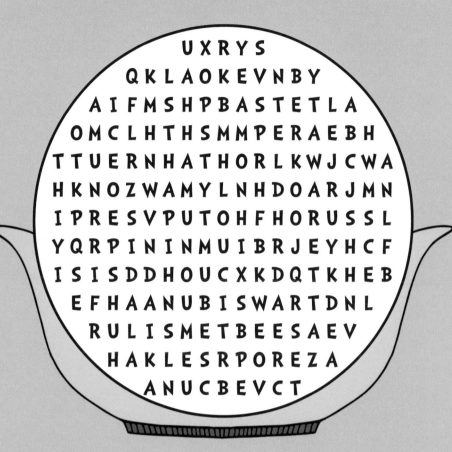

```
        U X R Y S
      Q K L A O K E V N B Y
    A I F M S H P B A S T E T L A
    O M C L H T H S M M P E R A E B H
    T T U E R N H A T H O R L K W J C W A
    H K N O Z W A M Y L N H D O A R J M N
    I P R E S V P U T O H F H O R U S S L
    Y Q R P I N I N M U I B R J E Y H C F
    I S I S D D H O U C X K D Q T K H E B
    E F H A A N U B I S W A R T D N L
    R U L I S M E T B E E S A E V
    H A K L E S R P O R E Z A
      A N U C B E V C T
```

Funny mummies

Where do mummies go on holiday?
The Dead Sea.

How do mummies hide?
They wear masking tape.

How do you use an Ancient Egyptian doorbell?
Toot and come in (Tutankhamun).

What kind of music do mummies like?
Wrap music.

Source material

The scribe has written a list of some things you can make from papyrus, a reed-like plant that grows along the Nile River. Check the list and work out which pictures are missing.

Paper

Basket

Sandals

Rope

Clothes

Boat

Food

Perfume

At the oasis

Can you spot five differences between these two pictures?

Fading beauty

Queen Nefertiti is fading away! Draw around her outlines, then color her in, too.

Flower power

Match the lotus blossom to the silhouette in the circle.

Mammoth monument

Which is the highest obelisk? Do the math to find out, then color them in if you like.

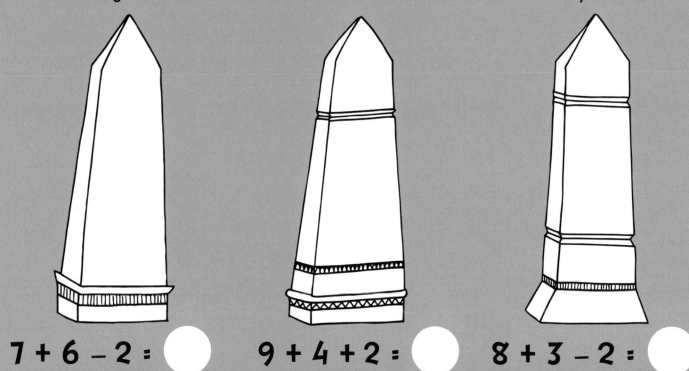

7 + 6 − 2 = ◯   9 + 4 + 2 = ◯   8 + 3 − 2 = ◯

Carved code

The Rosetta Stone has a code that explains the meaning of hieroglyphics.
Follow the tangled lines to see which Egyptologist will find it.

How to make a mummy

You'll need:

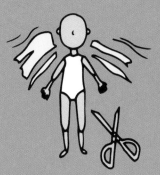

1 old doll

1 cup of water

old wooden spoon

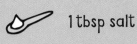

1 tbsp salt

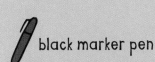

1 cup of flour

black marker pen

scissors

white fabric strips or paper, about ½in wide and 4in long

large mixing bowl

Ask a grown-up to help!

1. Cut as much hair off the doll as possible to make the mummy easier to wrap.

2. Mix the flour, water, and salt in a large mixing bowl to create a smooth paste.

3. Dip a strip of fabric or paper into your paste and squeeze gently to remove any excess. Now wrap the strip around the mummy as tightly as you can and repeat until the whole body is covered.

4. Leave to dry for 1 to 2 days. If you want to add another layer of bandages, it needs to be completely dry before you do so.

5. Use the marker pen to draw on eyes and a mouth.

Beastly business

How many of the following beasties can you find in the pharaoh's burial chamber?

Scarab beetles = ◯

Rats = ◯

Frogs = ◯

Scorpions = ◯

Dotty mummy cases

Join the two sets of dots to reveal the mummy cases, then color them in.

Meet the pharaoh (page 4)

Battle scene counting (page 9)

Bows = 2
Arrows = 6
Battle axes = 4
Daggers = 5

Tall order (page 9)

3   4   1   2   5

Odd Osiris out (page 5)

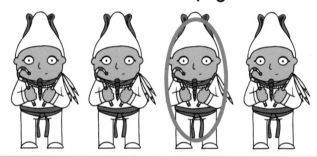

Work it out (page 5)

FARMER   SLAVE   SOLDIER   PRIEST   SCRIBE

Hidden in the pyramid (page 12)

Great gods (pages 6–7)

Isis   Horus   Thoth   Bastet   Anubis   Osiris

Dog differences (page 12)

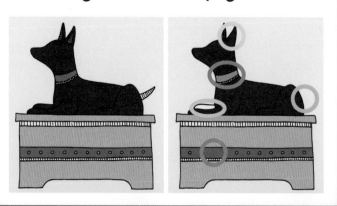

Chariot math (page 13)

Odd beetle out (page 13)

Tomb raider (page 15)

Find the lost tomb (page 16)

Mystery case (page 17)

The tape measure is missing.

Soldiering on (page 18)

Odd shields out (page 18)

Animal pairs (page 19)

Top of the pile (page 19)

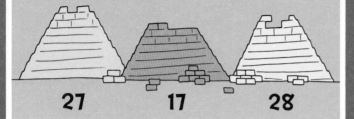

27   17   28

Recycled letters (page 20)

tomb	curse
scribe	slave
pyramid	flail

Muddled animal gods (page 21)

crocodile	falcon
cat	baboon
jackal	hippopotamus

Cattle counting (page 21)

Cattle = 12   Horns = 24

Secret message (page 25)

Dear Mark Antony,

How are you? It's been ages since we met. I think Octavian wants a fight because the Roman fleet has been spotted off the coast.

Please bring as many ships as you can and come quickly!

Love, Cleo

Game play (page 27)

Plain sailing (page 29)

7   4   14

Market dash (page 29)

Dance differences (page 30)

Musical mayhem (page 31)

On the menu (page 31)

```
R M U C L K R U X R Y S T M C A R N O
B H O N E Y P L C A A F I S H P B Y X
V I B E Y R F M Y S T S T D E L A R E
C P D D L H J N G N N S T H E E K H T
K K L S E T G F I O E B H U S S B O A
O L I W N V R N Z P V G R I E N W H S
R L M S T B S I F I G S J F M X A E S
Y Q R P I N A F P O E A E K B Y B J L
D S H O L L G N U C X K L Q K R K A D
A E G G S A E K J Y M F O W T E T F A
E M E Q I T S N B T B E E R A E V I T
T B J S G X G F E R P O R E Z A M U E
U L K G A R L I C Z A S B R E A D N S
```

Weighing it up (page 37)

♥ 27

♥ 20

♥ 14

Temple run (page 38)

Odd cats out (page 38)

Ceremonial dress up (page 39)
2 are wearing animal skins.

The write stuff (page 39)

Making a mummy (page 41)

The needle and thread are missing from the picture.

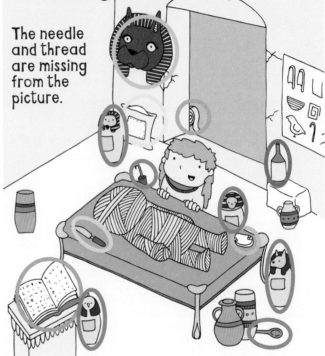

Stop, thief! (page 42)

61

Hidden in the picture (page 43)

Name game (page 44)

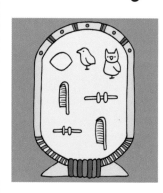 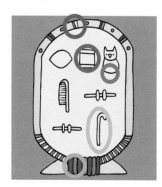

Twin charms (page 44)

Journey through the Underworld (page 46)

Heavy weights (page 47)

18

15

24

High society (page 47)

Gods wordsearch (page 51)

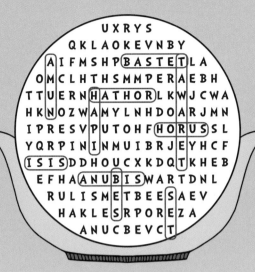

Source material (page 52)

Clothes and food are missing from the pictures.

At the oasis (page 52)

Flower power (page 53)

This one is the matching flower.

Mammoth monument (page 54)

11   15   9

Carved code (page 54)

Beastly business (page 56)

Scarab beetles = 3
Rats = 7
Frogs = 6
Scorpions = 3

First published 2019 by Button Books, an imprint of Guild of Master Craftsman Publications Ltd, Castle Place, 166 High Street, Lewes, East Sussex, BN7 1XU, UK. Text © GMC Publications Ltd, 2019. Copyright in the Work © GMC Publications Ltd, 2019. Illustrations © 2019 Jennifer Alliston. ISBN 978 1 78708 037 9. Distributed by Publishers Group West in the United States. All rights reserved. The right of Jennifer Alliston to be identified as the illustrator of this work has been asserted in accordance with the Copyright, Designs, and Patents Act 1988, sections 77 and 78. No part of this publication may be reproduced, stored in a retrieval system or transmitted in any form or by any means without the prior permission of the publisher and copyright owner. While every effort has been made to obtain permission from the copyright holders for all material used in this book, the publishers will be pleased to hear from anyone who has not been appropriately acknowledged and to make the correction in future reprints. The publishers and author can accept no legal responsibility for any consequences arising from the application of information, advice or instructions given in this publication. A catalog record for this book is available from the British Library. Publisher: Jonathan Bailey. Production: Jim Bulley and Jo Pallett. Senior Project Editor: Sara Harper. Managing Art Editor: Gilda Pacitti. Color origination by GMC Reprographics. Printed and bound in China. Warning! Choking hazard—small parts. Not suitable for children under 3 years.